THE PEACE OF FERRARA

Plays by Philip Merivale

KNUT AT ROESKILDE
THE WIND OVER THE WATER
THE PEACE OF FERRARA

The Peace of Ferrara

Drama in Three Acts by Philip Merivale

BOSTON
THE FOUR SEAS COMPANY
PUBLISHERS

ISBN: 978-1-4344-1338-3

The Four Seas Press
Boston, Mass., U.S.A.

To My Mother

THE PEACE OF FERRARA

DRAMATIS PERSONÆ

NICCOLO D'ESTE	*Marquis of Ferrara*
UGO D'ESTE	*His illegitimate son*
GIACOMO	
PARISINA D'ESTE	*Wife of Niccolo*
PELLEGRINA	
LUCIA	*Her maids*
LAODAMIA ROMEI	

TIME: 14—

The Peace of Ferrara

ACT I.   NICCOLO

*A small room in the Castle Tedaldo, Ferrara. At the
back a heavily curtained door leads to a large hall.
On the left a small door leads to a staircase.
A heavy oak table and chair are the chief features in
the furnishing of the room which is sombre and
lighted by a narrow lancet in the wall on the left.
There is a lamp on the table at which the Marquis
Niccolo is kneeling. Presently he rises and strikes
a bell. Giacomo enters by the private door on the
left.*

NICCOLO

That woman!

GIACOMO

Are you sick, my lord?

NICCOLO

Not now.

I have prayed. Go, bring her!
*(Giacomo goes out by the door. Niccolo stands
motionless till he re-enters with Laodamia Romei.
Giacomo retires. Niccolo seems unaware of the
woman's presence till she speaks.)*

LAODAMIA

Well! what would you of me?

[9]

NICCOLO

You are forgiven. Go, and sin no more!

LAODAMIA

Who claims to have forgiven me?

NICCOLO

                                    I have held
Debate with your offended lord, and sought
Council of God: lastly my lady's prayers
I have remembered, which more weighed with me
Than aught else in my judgment. I say therefore
You are forgiven. Go, and sin no more.

LAODAMIA

Go whither? To my husband?

NICCOLO

                              Ay to him
Whom you have injured past all hope of grace,
But whom, despite his lawful indignation
I have prevailed upon to pardon you.

LAODAMIA

Take back your pardon, both! I'll none of it!
I have assurances of mine own heart
That scorn the judgment of your courts—deny
Your right to pardon.

NICCOLO

                    What—can you reject
My mercy?

LAODAMIA

          Mercy call you it? To send
My body back to him that most offends
My soul?

NICCOLO

Body and soul have you offended
And were in danger soul and body too.
The punishment that lay within my power
By the old law that visits your offence,
Adultery, with death, by mine own power
I have this day remitted so you might
Deserve salvation ere you come to die.
Go! Get you to that work!

LAODAMIA

If I be damned
What's that to thee? I pay the penalty;
And for my lover hold damnation cheap.

NICCOLO

You know not what you say!

LAODAMIA

You have forgot
The speech of lovers! Then, if I be damned,
Who gave my body to the soul I loved,
Where groans the mother of your bastard now
Whom you desire to reign here after you?
(*Niccolo is shaken with the intensity of his fury but
says nothing.*)
I fear you not though you do gnaw that lip
Which hath spoke death as easily as it dealt
Kisses. I dare speak freely having thrown
Your pardon in your face.

NICCOLO

You know me not.
You shall not refuse pardon, for my heart

[11]

Shall follow you with peace though you oppose
Against me all the armoury of your hate.

LAODAMIA

It shall grow weary if it follow me.

NICCOLO

It may grow weary but it shall not rest
Till your proud heart be moved. This is my work,
Since for the guilt wherewith my youth was stained
God hath seen fit to heap mine age with joys,
I do perceive the work required of me.
I must not of my city lose one soul:
As mine own soul henceforth I must regard
All souls within my territories born.
So God remove my happiness from me
And make me for their guilt responsible
If by my fault one instant out of all
Eternity be lost to any here.

LAODAMIA

This new resolve circles too wide about
For its first flight. Begin in your own heart!

NICCOLO

I have begun there.

LAODAMIA

           And in your own house.
(*Enter Parisina d'Este by the door on the left.*)

PARISINA

Pardon me, sir!

NICCOLO

           Nay—do not go. What seek you?

[12]

PARISINA

To see if Ugo were with you—

NICCOLO

Is he come?

What? Is he here then?

PARISINA

Nay, my lord, not yet,
Unless he had been with you—I have sought elsewhere.
(*Laodamia laughs*)

NICCOLO

I can await the day your laughter shall
Be stilled in presence of my lovers here,
(*Taking Parisina's hand*)
By whom my house is placed above mischance.
Therefore, unhappy woman, seek again
In thy lord's bosom that deep love which makes
The soul impenetrable to disaster.

LAODAMIA

God's curse be mine if ever I do seek
Comfort or health of him. If love I need
I'll find it in that youth's delightful arms
You have banished in your dotard's righteousness.

NICCOLO

(*To Parisina*)

Be not afraid. This woman found in sin
Refuses pardon. But I am resolved
She shall return and on a broken heart
Refound the habitation of her soul.
Go to her, sweet! Bid her repent!

[13]

PARISINA

(*Going to her reluctantly*)

Alas!

LAODAMIA

I am not guilty if my heart approves.

NICCOLO

That way all sin were innocent.

LAODAMIA

The world
Were innocent could it but have my heart.

NICCOLO

I will not hear your blasphemy. Go forth
To him you have wronged; and that all men may mark
How I am bent to purify the world
I will send with you her that is to me
The revelation of God's love. Go, sweet!
Conduct her home.

PARISINA

Is it your will?

NICCOLO

It is.
Her life is yours since that your pray'rs outweighed
The law prescribing death for her offence.
So by your pray'rs her soul is respited.

PARISINA

Will you come with me, madam?

LAODAMIA

Fear you not
Contamination for her in my touch?

[14]

NICCOLO

When I fear that I will believe that death
Can overtake the everlasting soul.

(*Again Laodamia laughs and suffers Parisina to lead
her out by the private door. Niccolo watches them
and strikes the bell. Giacomo enters by private
door.*)

GIACOMO

I am glad to see you better.

NICCOLO

                A good deed done
Is physic to the body as to the soul.

GIACOMO

Why, any deed is medicine to a mind
Distracted with unwelcome thoughts.

NICCOLO

                   You speak
By old prescriptions.

GIACOMO

         New or old, good—evil
Are empty terms. I know not how to use them.

NICCOLO

That is a fault. Bitterly I have learnt
Evil, and God hath showered His good on me.
I have despatched my lady to restore
Laodamia Romei to her house.
Why do you shake your head?

GIACOMO

              Some women be
That have been harlots in their hearts from birth,

[15]

Who yet escape the act that names them so.
These may die young by grace of Providence,
With bodies undishonour'd be interr'd;
But others live till Time and Circumstance
Contrive the fell conjunction where such hearts
Inevitably must flower out in to sin.
And such was she that went but now from here.

NICCOLO

(*Laughing*)

Oh, you are wise. Where learnt you this?

GIACOMO

Mine eyes
Were first instructed by your lordship's self
To fix upon the heart beneath the breast;
Since when I have never closed them, but have seen
More it may be than e'er my master look'd for.

NICCOLO

(*Laughing*)

I am too old to wish a woman harm
Or I would counsel you to take a wife,
And learn the truth of women.

GIACOMO

I speak only
With my inferior wit.

NICCOLO

Enough. No news
Of the Count yet?

GIACOMO

No, my lord.

[16]

NICCOLO

                              Said he not
"Noon" in his message?

GIACOMO

            Yes.

NICCOLO

                         'Tis almost night.

GIACOMO

You fear no harm for him?

NICCOLO

                    I do believe
The darkest nature and the worst intent
Should brighten and to nobler ways be turned
By the brave invocation of his smile.

GIACOMO

'Twere most ironical should his father's son
Inherit nothing of the general peace
Your Highness has conferr'd on Italy.

NICCOLO

Giacomo, if I might tonight bequeath
To this unhappy land such peace as reigns
At last within my bosom, it were well
I should die now. Yet I shall live to see it!
Peace upon Italy!

GIACOMO

                The envoys, sir,
Of Venice take their leave of us tonight.

NICCOLO

Bring them together where I may bestow
My gifts upon them. Ha! You shake your head.
Again your judgment disapproves my work.
Well, where do you dispute it?

GIACOMO

                  Sir, I think
Such gifts unnecessary; and in the work
Of politics all superfluity
Is wasted power.

NICCOLO

(*Laughing*)

          To think I was your master
In this same art! And now do you presume
To teach me those old precepts I have striven
To banish from the world. You are grown old,
Giacomo.

GIACOMO

        I at least have not returned
To infancy.

NICCOLO

       True, my heart's lighter now
Than it has been these forty years, my friend.

GIACOMO

You give too much to Venice. You expose
Too warm a love to Rimini and Rome.
Take heed lest your affections presently
Betray you where you most have put your trust.

NICCOLO

I am content to hazard with my life
My new idea of man: and I will show

[18]

My heart to Italy and pour out my love
On all that were at enmity with me.
If these betray me—let them have the forfeit;
For life shall have no value any more.
But love and faith were never yet bestowed
On man or woman but the gift in time
Made gracious giver and receiver too.
Therefore I seek no nobler name than this,
Who am called "The Peacemaker of Italy."
Am I not praised already?

GIACOMO

If I kept
Chickens I'd praise the fox who pared his nails
And had his teeth drawn for the love of God.
When you were called "The Leopard" men drew breath
Securely in Ferrara. Now you spread
Wings like a dove and pout your breast-feathers,
Some of our sentry-spirits have no sleep.

NICCOLO

I shall disarm the world. Tomorrow goes
My lady to her father at Rimini,
To seal our treaty by her presence.—Well?

GIACOMO

My lady rides at noon?

NICCOLO

No. Earlier.
It was my son should have arrived at noon.
My lady starts at dawn, or not long after.

GIACOMO

Ay, that is better.

[19]

NICCOLO

Why? You knew the hour.
Were you not present when 'twas so arranged?

GIACOMO

I had forgotten, or was may be confused
By the Count's message: then if Ugo stay
A few hours longer he will come too late
To bid her farewell.

NICCOLO

And it were a pity;
For she, I know, will grieve as much as he.

GIACOMO

I am not sorry.

NICCOLO

What?

GIACOMO

'Tis better so.

NICCOLO

Why do you say that? Do you hate to see
Happiness in the young as well as old?

GIACOMO

Sir, I may claim to be indifferent
To happiness or unhappiness, in age
Or youth. I seek not pleasure out of life,
And pain extorts no protest out of me.
My life hath but one function—to promote
The welfare of the State, as I discern it,
And to fustrate the schemes of others. Such
Am I, your servant, a machine contrived
By men's necessities for a thousand years,

And as you shall employ it you shall find
Reliable, loyal, indispensable.

NICCOLO

Now be not you deceived. 'Tis time to speak;
For the division I have lately marked
Between our councils is more deeply set
Than I at first was willing to believe.
But I can spare you, be assured of that
More easily than you think.—But come! Enough
Of difference and division, since tonight
Ugo comes home after a year away.
Is it not strange, old heathen, after a life
Tempestuous more than most, God should reward
My age with such a wife and such a son?
This should plant grace in *you*.

GIACOMO

                        I have heard it said
That Rimini's daughter and Ferrara's son
Were better matched in years than she and you.

NICCOLO

Why, so they were, being each a child, no more
When first I brought her hither.

GIACOMO

                         But this year—

NICCOLO

Well?

GIACOMO

    And not once alone I have heard it, too;
And now they are no more children.

NICCOLO

Now—take care!
Do not you seek the old Italian way
To nerve your failing hold upon my councils
By sowing venom of domestic strife
In *this* house! Let not service flatter you!
Close in my secret mind though you have lived
Yet as we root out of our very hearts
Those thoughts that in infected sleep achieve
The recognition which our waking hours
Disdain to give them—so without remorse
Will I destroy and blacken from my mind,
Silence the lips, and still the envious brain
That should conceive and utter calumny
Against the innocence of these I love.

GIACOMO

I see my counsel is no more required.
I see the end of that estate wherein
My poor abilities have served you, sir.
We live in different worlds and I in one
Of vile mortality, that hath in it
Evil and hatred, envy and cruelty
And no experience that might benefit
The perfect planet where your lordship dwells.
Give leave that I retire, then, from your court
Till Time redeem my credit.

NICCOLO

As you please.

GIACOMO

The world's wide and the field for mischief lies
Outside these walls.

[22]

NICCOLO

Then there's your place.

GIACOMO

I claim it.

(*Enter by the private door Ugo Aldobrandino d'Este.
He is travel-stained. He hesitates on the threshold.
Niccolo rushes to embrace him.*)

NICCOLO

What! Are you come? At last! Nay do not kneel!
We looked for you at noon. Why came you not?
Your mother well-nigh wept—she went but now—
No matter whither—shortly she'll be back.
She will rejoice—Giacomo, will she not?—
To find thee here—at last!

GIACOMO

Ay. By your leave
I will assemble the ambassadors.

NICCOLO

Do so. And hark! Those sharp words we exchanged
Are quite forgotten. Come! A general peace
To celebrate his coming!

GIACOMO

As for me
I will forget; but that will not remove
The causes of the difference between us.

NICCOLO

You are old—you are old and hard to please, my friend.
Get hence to what you better understand
And leave us to our joy

(*Exit Giacomo by centre doors.*)

[23]

These grey bachelors
Are dangerous: they draw the wrath of God
Upon us by their faces and sour speech.
Ugo! My son! Well, have you lost your voice?
Nothing to say after a year?

UGO

Indeed
I know not how to tell you—

NICCOLO

Well, it needs
No long premeditation to exclaim
"Home! Father! Mother!"

(*He embraces him again*)

Son—my son—my son!
I have a thing to tell you. I have spent
The long year of your absence worthily
How, think you?

UGO

Nay, I know not.

NICCOLO

Guess then—guess!

UGO

Indeed I cannot.

NICCOLO

Yes—to please me! Come!

UGO

My lord, indeed I cannot.

NICCOLO

Then I'll tell you.
I have secured by favour of the Pope

Your claim to the succession after me
And your legitimacy recognized.

UGO

How can I thank you for a gift, my lord,
That only by your death can be enjoyed?

NICCOLO

Nay, thank me not; for this was my delight
And long-neglected duty, since by me,
By mine own fault your birth encumbered was
And still the debt increased as year by year
Your life hath been my blessing.

UGO

                      But I fear
Lest I should prove unworthy.

NICCOLO

                      Fear not that!
This is no burden that you cannot bear
Easily. Clear those shadows from your face!
What is it that oppresses you?

UGO

                      My lord,
You know I love you—

NICCOLO

                      Now I know you seek
A favour. Ask it! Nothing in my gift
Will I deny you.

UGO

                    Let me go away—
As far as I have been—as long again!

[25]

NICCOLO

What must I think of this? Albeit it needs
No long deliberation to reply.
How often did you slight my messages
Bidding you home again? and only at last
Were brought unwillingly obedient
Upon a firm command! And now you ask
To go away again! What should I think?

UGO

Not that I love you not!

NICCOLO

                        But that you love
Some other better?

UGO

                Can you think that? Why?

NICCOLO

Because I was a young man in my youth.

UGO

Sire, have I your leave once more to travel?
I have much to learn of people.

NICCOLO

                            This wish only
I have much pleasure in denying you.

UGO

I wish I might persuade you.

NICCOLO

                        Nay, you shall not.

UGO

I pray you—let me go!

NICCOLO

I will not. There.

UGO

I must obey.

NICCOLO

Be not down-cast at it!
It is my love commands your presence here;
You never found it a hard task-master.
Come, let me see you smile! So wintrily?
Like the reflection of the moon on ice.
(*After a silence Niccolo puts his arm round Ugo's neck.*)
Tell me the reason you desire to leave me—
Some woman somewhere? Tell me who she is!
Some girl—a briar-rose in an English lane?
Or lily from the court of France? No matter.
Between these two Ferrara's heir may choose
Whate'er his eye may fancy. Tell me now!
None is so willing, none so capable
To help you to your heart's desire as I.

UGO

Father—!

NICCOLO

Why—what's the need of mystery?
You shall be happy in your heart's desire.

UGO

God grant there come no sorrow out of it.
(*Parisina enters by the private way.*)

NICCOLO

Ah! Here's your consolation, or your grief
Were inconsolable.

[27]

PARISINA

You are come at last!

(*Ugo kisses her hand formally.*)

NICCOLO

What penance shall we set him for those tears
You shed when he came not this afternoon?

UGO

You wept, madam?

PARISINA

Ah no, indeed I did not.

NICCOLO

Ay that you did and said you had good cause
Since well your woman's intuition knew
Some evil had befallen him, which I,
Being but a dull-brained man, could not divine.
Believe me, son, she wept.

UGO

I am ashamed
To have caused you any sorrow.

NICCOLO

But I think
Your long delay hath hurt your mother less
Than your desire to leave us wounded me.

PARISINA

Leave us again?

NICCOLO

Ay, yonder caitiff, madam,
Is but a prisoner on my arrest.
And since a tyrant may detain the flesh

But not the heart—his heart is far away,
A prisoner too in voluntary bonds
More delicate than mine.

PARISINA

It is not so?

NICCOLO

But who this mistress is or where she dwells
He will not tell me. Do you discover it,
Parisina.

PARISINA

Is it so?

(*Ugo turns away*)

NICCOLO

Nay—before me

He is dumb. Now, while I speed the messengers
Of Venice on their journey—press him—press him.
Surprise his secret.

(*He turns to go*)

UGO

(*Vehemently*)

Father—do not go!

NICCOLO

Son.

UGO

Give me leave to go!

NICCOLO

This wound is deep?

Like an ill-mannered audience have I laughed
At a scene of genuine passion? You must pardon

[29]

An old man that with passions long outworn
Forgets the bitterness of love to youth.
Tell me your grief.
(*Giacomo enters by the curtained door in the center.
A murmur is heard from the hall behind.*)

GIACOMO

      Sir, the ambassadors—
I'll say you cannot come.

NICCOLO

        Nay, but I will.
(*Giacomo retires. Again the murmur.*)
How nearly for a private grief I came
To stinting public service. While I am gone,
Madam, unmask the lovely mystery
That holds his fancy far from home and us.
(*He smiles at them and goes out through the curtains.*)

PARISINA

It is not true.

UGO

      What shall I say?

PARISINA

          A woman
Kept you so long away, and makes you now
Impatient of us—vext at heart, because
Our love demands attention that your heart
Would fain keep undivided for another!

UGO

Nay, that's not so.

PARISINA

Will you deny it now?
Is't not the way of lovers to begrudge
Ev'n due affection elsewhere?

UGO

                              If it be
Yet am I not so.

PARISINA

                    Wherefore came you in, then,
At nightfall when we look'd for you at noon.
Why came you home at all?

UGO

                              Oh, you mistake me.
It is not so.

PARISINA

                    Say it a thousand times
And you shall not persuade me.   Come—her name!

UGO

I never may reveal it.

PARISINA

                    Then it is true!
Why must you lie?   Yet tell me but her name!
You will not?

UGO

          By the help of God I will not.

PARISINA

I go away tomorrow.

UGO

                    Go away!
Whither?

[31]

To Rimini to my father's house.

(*A silence*)

Farewell.

UGO

(*Vehemently*)

Ay, well it is! And fare you well,
Madam.

PARISINA

'Tis only for a little while.
You that have been a year away and felt
No pangs of separation need not fear
So short an absence.

UGO

Ere you have returned
I shall be gone.

PARISINA

It will be autumn then,
The season that our childhood most enjoyed.
Clear cold mornings, red leaf, and the nights
Descending suddenly, such brief evenings,—
Too brief if never more to come for us.
Last year you had just left us—the first time
Since I came hither—'twas the first I spent
The afternoons of autumn all alone.
This year I thought to live the past again
All as it was before.

UGO

When we would sit
In the deep window seat and read together—

PARISINA

Oh! you remember!

UGO

        Or tell fairy-tales
Wherein folk loved and suffered without grief
Being but fabrications of a dream:
How many years ago?

PARISINA

        Not two—not two.
'Tis not so distant but we may recall
Our childhood's happiness—if you will stay
Till I come back.

UGO

        'Tis useless to contrive
A snare for future happiness. If life
Will bring the old days back and the young hearts
Revive in us, the miracle will be wrought
Without our preparation.

PARISINA

        Dare you trust
To Time, the jester who delights to grant
Our wishes when desire for them is dead?
What if he brings us back the hours we love
When we are wiser and no more can be
Content with old romances!

UGO

        That's the fear!
Lest we have grown too wise and left behind
The sweet content of children with a tale,—
And on our souls fall guilt of—

[33]

(They stand in silence, looking upon each other; she stretches out her hand and touches him.)

PARISINA

Ugo—Ugo!
Was it for this you stayed away from me?

UGO

Yes. How long have you known this in your heart?

PARISINA

Since you have been away. But I believe
It was my heart's joy in another world.

UGO

Dare we believe that?

PARISINA

Do you not remember
The day we met? I see the flowers—the spears—
And you on a white horse to welcome me—
And then I prayed, even then I know I prayed,
Even then that you should love me—even then!

(They are very close—and very still.)

UGO

I will go.

PARISINA

Can you?

UGO

Let me go before
This moment lose its bliss.

PARISINA

Why now—why now?
Where shall you 'scape? This moment is the crown
Of countless ages. The flower that blooms but now
Had long ago its sowing.

[34]

UGO

Yet I will go
Before one leaf or petal of it fall.
(*Niccolo enters through the curtains unperceived.*)

PARISINA

I see that we are grown up with this world
And never can be children any more.

NICCOLO

(*Fiercely*)

Children?
What have you suffered in your lives, or what
Harsh intimations have your dreams divulged
That you should wish for childhood back again?

UGO

My lord—does not the happiest man regret
Sometimes his childhood?

NICCOLO

Nay, not such as you.
If life had brought you sorrow, sin, remorse—
But you twain in your cherished lives—each day
Attended by devotion—what have you
Learned to regret?

UGO

It is an idle word
Which many use without cause—

NICCOLO

Where—where—where?
There's more in this. Who, in your hearing, spake
This idle word?

(*Enter Giacomo*)

[35]

No longer children—you—
Never again!
(*He catches sight of Giacomo and controls himself.*)
Nay, do not be dismayed.
Sometimes I pay for peace in mine old age
By these recurrent storms, the muttering
Of that subsiding tempest of my life:
Spent thunder.

(*He staggers*)

GIACOMO

Come, sir, sit!

NICCOLO

I am not so old
That a day's work toward evening wearies me.
No, I'll not sit.

(A *silence*)

At what hour of the morning
Do you set out for Rimini, my lady?

PARISINA

Soon after dawn.

NICCOLO
(*to Ugo*)

You are weary, are you not?
Not fit to take a journey?

UGO

Nay, my lord.
Give me but your permission. I am ready
To take my travels up again.

NICCOLO

That's well.
Tomorrow you shall start for Rimini
With her.

[36]

UGO

My lord—

NICCOLO

Enough.

UGO

Father—

NICCOLO

I say
You shall! For I desire, madam, to show
The Malatesta's daughter honour. Therefore
My dearest treasure, this my darling heir,
Shall grace your retinue. Make ready both.
(*The two go out, Parisina by the private way. Ugo
through the curtained door in the center.*)

NICCOLO

Give me that chair.
(*Giacomo pushes the chair toward him.*)
I am faint: not old—not old.
If I were old I might feel jealousy
But that's a thing I know not.

GIACOMO

What's amiss, sir?

NICCOLO

You—you! 'Twas you that in a damned hour
Distilled a poison from a pleasant word—
Children! You saw these twain that yesterday
Were children? Truth and beauty are corrupt
For ever and the firmament above us
Leans on crack'd pillars if the fear you have raised
Be not at once disproved. Go with them, therefore,

[37]

These children, on their journey. Watch for me.
I tell you not what you shall look to find.
I charge them not. Be you not over-zealous;
Be not deceived. Mistake them not, I charge you.
Death is amongst us. Where the lie is found
The liar shall be silenced—be it yourself
Or who it may. Watch them, and report
Truthfully, instantly and wholly. Go!
(*Giacomo takes leave by the private door, a smile on his lips. Niccolo draws his dagger in a frenzy and stabbing it into the table falls on his knees before the cross so made.*)
And God! In mercy see the truth be fair
And the whole Truth as Thy Son innocent!

CURTAIN

ACT II.

ACT II. GIACOMO

Room at an inn on the road to Rimini. Two doors are
in the left-hand wall, the lower one leading directly
to another room; the upper one to the passage and
stairs. High up in the right hand wall is another
door leading to a bedroom. Two small windows are
set deep in the ramp of the roof which descends
upon the back wall, cutting it short and diminishing
the size of the room. The furniture is scanty and
rough. There is a table low down towards the left
with wooden chairs behind and at each end of it.
A long settee or couch is placed near the right hand
wall. Giacomo is seated at the table with his back
to Pellegrina who is standing at the window towards
the right. Lucia is standing at the foot of the table,
in the centre of the room.

GIACOMO

This I have read is your sworn deposition.

LUCIA

I swore to nothing, sir.

GIACOMO

You are on oath.

I told you that.

LUCIA

I did not think—

[41]

GIACOMO

　　　　　　I am sorry.
I put it plainly to you. You are to blame.
You have no more to tell us?

LUCIA

　　　　No, sir.

GIACOMO

　　　　　　　　Come.
Sign it.
(*She approaches timidly. He gives her a pen and
watches her closely as she signs.*)
　　　The hand is poor but good enough
To damn you if you lie.

LUCIA

　　　　　　　I swear I knew not
That I was swearing.

GIACOMO

　　　From this evidence
What inference have you drawn?
　　　　(*She stares stupidly*)
　　　　　　　　I say, to what
Conclusion are you forced, then?

LUCIA

　　　　　　Why, to nothing
But what I have already told you, sir.

GIACOMO

I see you are a fool. Get you within.
　　(*Lucia goes out by the lower door on the left.*)
Come, niece! Please God your wits are sound. I grow

Impatient of the fools that walk the world.
And times are ticklish for us when the wise
Are put in peril of our precious heads
By dolts and dotards. We are of one blood, though,
And understand each other's genius, eh?

And yet may not agree.

GIACOMO
                    Well said! Well said!
Now is there aught you'll contradict in this?
Nay—wait! I'll not commit you hastily
To any statement. I will read once more
The evidence of yonder fool. Sit down.
(*Pellegrina sits in the chair at the left of the table,
her back to the door by which Lucia went out.*)
"At first my lord rode by my lady's side.
His head was bowed. He did not speak at all.
My lady sought to cheer him, but in vain.
After we left the town he fell behind.
Twice she sent for him, but he would not come.
My lady grieved at this." The witness swears
That entering this inn "My lady sent
Once more to bring him to her; still in vain.
At this she wept." Now is there aught in this
You would change?

PELLEGRINA
No, nothing.

GIACOMO
                    Do you sign it too, then.

PELLEGRINA
Why?

[43]

GIACOMO

For my lady's sake—for mine—for yours.
Lord Niccolo desired me make report
Of each day's happenings. This is innocent?
Do you not think so?

PELLEGRINA

Yes.

GIACOMO

Come sign it then.

(*Pellegrina signs*)

So there. That's good. And have you naught to add?

PELLEGRINA

Nothing.

GIACOMO

Come, think. I do not ask in jest.
Do not dismiss it lightly.

(*She shakes her head*)

Very well.
Now, what conclusion do you draw from this?

PELLEGRINA

(*Contemptuously*)

I will not say what you would have me say.

GIACOMO

Then you perceive what I suspected. Good.

PELLEGRINA

Do not assume too much.

GIACOMO

Come, come! Speak out!

[44]

PELLEGRINA

I will say nothing: what from that you infer
Be it at your own peril.

GIACOMO

Body of God!
Was ever man so put to it before?
To drive two stubborn mares in the one yoke,
Folly and Virtue! One without the wit
To see aught worth the telling: and yourself
That see, but will not for your virtue speak!

PELLEGRINA

Were all men of your mind 'twere a sick world
For honesty to dwell in.

GIACOMO

I do not see
'Tis anything but evil as it is.
But what of that? We are philosophers—
Both. I repent I have so long deferred
My duty to my kinswoman. From now
I must bestir myself to your advancement.

PELLEGRINA

Tomorrow, sir.
            (*Suggesting that he should go*)

GIACOMO

I speak now to an armed
And ready intellect: that's not to say
You have not beauty enough to make your brains
Superfluous.

PELLEGRINA
            (*courtesying*)
Mercy, Uncle!
[45]

GIACOMO

(*producing letter*)

              I have here
A letter to my lord of Rimini,
My lady's father, to whose house we go.
This Malatesta is a prince as yet
Quite uninfected by the dove-cote-creed
That saps Ferrara. For his daughter's sake
I think the Lord of Rimini would rejoice
To stay our Christian haste to worldly ruin,
Though to that end he must remove the preacher
Of peace to Italy.

PELLEGRINA

               Not—not my lord—
Lord Niccolo!

GIACOMO

          Come—hold your peace! No names!
Now if, when I have spoken with your mistress
I bid you see my supper is prepared,
Go to the messenger that waits below
And bid him ride with this.

         (*She holds out her hand.*)

              Nay—in good time.
But—if I cry for cordial—then go down
To that same messenger, and bid him fetch
Lord Niccolo hither!

PELLEGRINA

Wherefore?

GIACOMO

             Because I think
My lady is sick, and I would therefore bring

[46]

Either her father or her husband hither
To find the remedy.

PELLEGRINA

How is she sick?

GIACOMO

I cannot tell till I have spoken with her;
And till I know I cannot be decided
If Rimini or Ferrara be the right
Prescription for her.

PELLEGRINA

This I will not do.
You have a deeper reason than her health
To bring her husband hither.

GIACOMO

Excellent!

PELLEGRINA

Why do you seek my help? A word from you
Would be sufficient.

GIACOMO

I'll be honest with you.
Know then, Lord Niccolo hath threaten'd me
With torture and with death if I mistake
In my suspicions—be they what they may.
Therefore I need a witness, and I seek
To implicate another in this work
For my own life's sake; and have chosen you
To share the danger and the privilege.

PELLEGRINA

Oh, thank you! I refuse it!

[47]

GIACOMO

Hear me out

I pray—But if you send the messenger
Yourself, my lord will know, you understand,
That you had reason, something to report.
You shall not then protest your ignorance
Of that which he shall question you upon.
And to make sure he comes—I leave you this
To give the messenger.

(*He hands her the deposition. She makes an angry
gesture of destroying it.*)

If you do so

Though I am somewhat shaken in my credit
I have sufficient favour with my lord
To have your throat cut and no forms of law
Omitted. What are you? I do not ask
For your approval. This is my command.

(*Parisina enters from her room on the right.*)

PELLEGRINA

Madam, have you not slept?

PARISINA

The room is full

Of shadows from the moon. How shall I sleep?

GIACOMO

I fear we rode too far. Rest on this couch.

(*She refuses*)

Shall we stop here a day or two?

PARISINA

I had rather

Die by the road.

[48]

GIACOMO

You will think differently
Tomorrow. Have you supp'd?

PARISINA

(*Sitting by the table*)

Oh, what is food
That they would have you eat when you are sad?

GIACOMO

But this can be no common weariness
If you will neither eat nor sleep.

(*He takes her hand*)

I have
Some skill in medicine. Ah! Your hand is cold.
Nay then, no fever.

(*He passes his hand over her forehead. She shakes
her head impatiently.*)

Something in the mind?
You are sick for home! A husband's love!

PARISINA

Your skill

In medicining the body-politic
Will not help human sickness.

GIACOMO

It may be so.
But you should wait to hear what I prescribe.
I see you are lonesome for familiar faces
And voices of your kindred. Here's my niece—;
I will not say that my familiar features
Are at your service to dispel your grief—
But Lucia is within: still you'll desire

[49]

One of your own blood who shall help create
Here in this inn illusions of your home.
But who, now, who can play this part for you?
I have it—why—the count—Ugo!

PARISINA

                                      He is not
Of my blood.

GIACOMO

                    None the less—quick, Pellegrina,
Bid the count hasten hither. Have I not
Some skill then? Why, the blood already creeps
Into your cheek again. And in your wrist
A tiny hammer beats against my palm.
A cure—confess!

PARISINA

                         You might as well prescribe
Gold from a sunbeam.

PELLEGRINA

                         Sir, my lady means
Count Ugo will not come. For more than once
She hath sent for him in vain.

GIACOMO

                              But tell him now
That I am with my lady to discuss
Urgent affairs committed to my charge
By my lord Niccolo, which he must hear.

PELLEGRINA

Uncle, it may be that the count has reason—
That he is sleeping or hath ridden on—

GIACOMO

But now I saw him dicing with the horse-boys—

PELLEGRINA

Yet even so—

PARISINA

Why do you stand and talk?
Do as your uncle bids you!
(*Pellegrina goes out unwillingly by the upper door on
the left.*)

GIACOMO

That is well.
I have thought often that Ferrara's lady,
Despite the gentleness that graces her,
Might show a little more authority
With them that wait on her.

PARISINA

Do not suppose
But I care nothing for authority.

GIACOMO

Madam, you must not say it. For we're come
On easy days; and government, I fear,
Errs toward a mildness that the world mistakes
For weakness. But 'tis late for lessons now.
Come: Let me place this pillow at your back.

PARISINA

I'll rest upon this couch.

GIACOMO

That's better; yes.
(*As he helps her across the room*)
Why, what a thing is youth! But suffer it
To have its way and it will find of nature
The cure physicians could not hit upon.

[51]

Here's naught amiss but rest shall set to rights
By morning.

(*He makes her comfortable and returns with a chair:
seating himself beside her he takes her hand.*)

PARISINA

Think you youth has in itself
The properties of healing?

GIACOMO

Surely it hath.

PARISINA

No matter what disease?

GIACOMO

I'll vouch for it.

PARISINA

You have the doctor's art of flattering
The hopes his patient hardly dare confess.

GIACOMO

And little else avails in medicine.
Trust me!

PARISINA

I will—till I feel worse again.

(*They laugh together*)

Strange how I always feared you! Now you are
My only comforter. Now I shall never
Fear you again. Where learned you all your skill
In medicine?

GIACOMO

Is it less to undertake
The surgery of state, a corporate life—
Than to prescribe but for a single body?

[52]

PARISINA

But there's a difference.

GIACOMO

Nay, the state's a body
Whereof we are the organs, limbs, veins, arteries.
For both we seek health, and in both alike
Combat disease.

PARISINA

I see. This *sounds* like wisdom.

GIACOMO

I would I might as easily persuade
Your husband. He protests my theories
Are outworn.

PARISINA

I will speak to him.

GIACOMO

Ay, do so.

For what's the letting of a little blood
For health's sake!

PARISINA

Blood!

GIACOMO

Surgery.

PARISINA

'Tis a jest
Among the wise to force comparisons
Beyond the bounds of folly. But I lack
The wit to relish such a jest, and pass
The horror of your implications by.

[53]

GIACOMO

(*smiling*)

But here's no cause for pity or dismay,
Anger or horror. Nay, it were a vice
For the preservation of a limb diseased
To let the body die.

PARISINA

(*laughing*)

I see how well
You love to prop your false presumptions up
With buttresses of soundest reasoning.
If you have quarrelled with my lord on this
He is to blame. Did he not laugh at it?

GIACOMO

(*smiling*)

Nay, but you must not laugh. All this is true.
When your lord's father slew his brother's son
Obizzo, some there were looked black at it.
But I perceive he sought the common health.

PARISINA

By murder?

(*She starts up in horror*)

GIACOMO

(*Replacing her pillow*)

Let me smooth if for you again.
(*He places the pillow very gently under her head.*)
That which we call a knife the surgeon calls
A lancet. Murder in the vulgar use
Is but the pricking of a festered place
In the state's body.

PARISINA

This is horrible.

GIACOMO

We surgeons need firm nerves to do the acts
Men rail at though to their own profit aimed.

PARISINA

I'd rather lose my share than profit so.

GIACOMO

(*smiling*)

You speak in haste. A generous feeling prompts
What facts and more reflection must retract.
For 'tis my sure conviction no man lives—
Nor woman neither, that would stick at crime
To prosper his advantage.

PARISINA

No—no—no.

GIACOMO

Be that advantage but enough desired.

PARISINA

Be the advantage Heaven—or what it may—
I would not—no—nor any that I know—
Consent to purchase it at such a price.

GIACOMO

But were you threatened in your dearest hope—
One plotted, say, against your dignity
As princess of Ferrara—would you not
Defend it?

PARISINA

What—by murder?

[55]

GIACOMO

                   How that word
Defeats all reason! But I had forgot;
You value not position. Well, suppose
Some attribute you valued, some possession
You would not part with—ay, or better still
Were there a thing you lacked and much desired
In life, from whose possession and enjoyment
You were obstructed by a tyrant's will—
You would not pause at his removal?

PARISINA

                          Yes.
I do not know the privilege I lack
That at such cost should seem desirable.

GIACOMO

And yet they tell a story of your race,
How Paolo that loved his brother's wife
Was by him slain. Now had the lovers killed
Count Malatesta that their love might bloom—
Nay! Do not start! I fear you breathe but hard
The thin air of pure reason. Had you been
Francesca, would not you for Paolo's love
Have sanctioned such a deed? Nay, would not you
Yourself have stabbed Giovanni rather—?

PARISINA

                     No—no—no!

GIACOMO

True, it had been a pity since that lord
Brought to his princely office noble gifts,
Iron in council as in war. But—

PARISINA

                What, then?

[56]

GIACOMO

But had his nerve grown feeble—
                              Well! What then?

GIACOMO

Why, like a skilled physician I deplore
Bloodshed, though where 'tis requisite I feel
No fear to use the knife. So had he been
Past service to the state I should have found
My duty in removing this dead limb
And giving freedom to the trunk to grow.

PARISINA

I cannot think how ever I was born
Of such a stock, nor what malicious fate
Hath wedded me into a house that groans
Under the burden of a kinsman's blood.
Yet is my lord gentle and merciful
And doth in this as much belie his race
As I do mine.

GIACOMO

                I know, madam, I know.
The peace of my lord's household hath become
The admiration of all Italy.
                (*After a silence*)
Madam, have you observed him lately?

PARISINA

                              Whom?

GIACOMO

My lord, your husband.

PARISINA
Why?

[57]

GIACOMO

Ah, then you have not.
That's strange. To me it seems most clear, and still
I think mine observation sure—I cannot
Be wrong. I cannot.

PARISINA

What have you observed?

GIACOMO

For some months past it hath appeared to me
What never could I have declared before,
That Niccolo, my lord, is growing old.
He speaks no longer with the vigorous tongue
Of the firm monarch he was wont to be.
I am sorry for it.

PARISINA

An evil none escapes
Is hardly an evil. You yourself are old.

GIACOMO

Not in my wits. Ferrara, as I think,
Needs young wits and young passions and the nerves
Of young hearts. Where could such an one be found
To share the burden and in time succeed
To the sole government. 'Twere natural
To name Count Ugo.

PARISINA

You dare not whisper it
But as in jest.

GIACOMO
(*sternly*)
Think on what I have said!

[58]

If one obstruct the progress of the state,
Reduce its health, threaten its sacred life,
He is an enemy of the common-wealth
And must, ere this should sicken, be cut off.

PARISINA

Ah! Ser Giacomo!

GIACOMO

Have you never thought,
Deep in your heart, that such your lord might be?
Hath none proposed it to you? None awaked
Within your soul a sympathetic stir
Of other passions, personal, not of state,
Which promised aid to such intents as this?

PARISINA

I dare not think what this should mean.

GIACOMO

Ha! Dare not?
We do not fear what never came to mind.
This possibility you have discern'd
Though from your thought you banished it.

PARISINA

Indeed
I cannot think—

GIACOMO

Briefly! Have you not dreamed,
Have you not in your bosom entertained
For whatsoever reason, a design
To kill your husband?

PARISINA
(*starting up*)
No! Upon my soul.

[59]

GIACOMO

(*almost thrusting her down*)

You never would by any influence
Of obligation to Ferrara's state
Or by some secret passion of your heart
Be to this act persuaded?

PARISINA

No! By God!

GIACOMO

Yet doing this your will henceforth should be
Paramount in Ferrara, and none living
Come between you and your desire on earth!

PARISINA

Never! Never!

GIACOMO

(*after a silence*)

Good. I am glad to hear
From you this refutation of a charge
That rumour hath already set afoot.

PARISINA

Of me, sir? To conspire against my lord?

GIACOMO

'Tis pointed more indeed at one we love,
Count Ugo. Yet your name is implicated,
Because 'tis thought your father Malatesta
Hath in your interest with the count contrived
Against your lord.

PARISINA

You know it cannot be,
That Ugo—

[60]

GIACOMO

I know this, that yesterday
The young man feared to meet his father's eyes,
Unwillingly came home and earnestly
Implored his leave to go away again.

PARISINA

But not for such a reason.

GIACOMO

You are right.
(*He rises*)
I thank you for correcting me.   I know
My course now.
    (*He burns the letter to Malatesta in the lamp*)
            It is good to be relieved
Of vile suspicions be they false or true.
To know one's course however hard it be
Is a kind of peace.

PARISINA

But do they say such things
Of Ugo?

GIACOMO

Nay, have comfort!   Fear you not.
Your soul is free of fault.

PARISINA

Of such a fault
God knows it hath been ever, though He see
What other sins deface it.

GIACOMO

Then be sure
No evil shall befall the innocent.

[61]

This night hath not unprofitably passed
Since we have found unfounded slander out.
(*Enter Pellegrina with Ugo by the upper door on left*)

PARISINA

Ugo! Oh, I am glad you have come.

UGO

I pray you
Be brief, Giacomo!
(*Giacomo staggers and leans upon a chair*)

PELLEGRINA
Uncle!

UGO
Why—what ails you?

GIACOMO
(*faintly*)

One moment!

PARISINA
Ser Giacomo!

GIACOMO
Pellegrina—
Some cordial!—quick.

PELLEGRINA
Uncle, I do beseech you—

GIACOMO

Cordial—

PELLEGRINA
God's pity, no!
(*Giacomo falls on the table*)

[62]

PARISINA

Pellegrina—quickly.
Bring cordial. Oh, be gone!
(*Pellegrina goes out*)

UGO

(*loosening Giacomo's collar*)
He's fainted.

PARISINA

Oh—

Tell me it is a lie—

UGO

Loose my arm, madam!

PARISINA

Say that they lie who charge you—

UGO

His eyelids moved.

PARISINA

Tell me—I know you never have contrived
Evil against—

UGO

Pray, madam, loose my arm.
I cannot help him—

PARISINA

Speak with me tonight—

UGO

Giacomo! Giacomo! Giacomo!

PARISINA

I must speak with you.

UGO

Have you no mercy?—this man's dying here!

[63]

PARISINA

I pray you do not chide me—nay—not you.
Better if he had died an hour ago
Before he put this horror in my soul.
           (*Re-enter Pellegrina with cordial.*)

UGO

Well done! Comes this fit often?

PELLEGRINA

No, I think not.

UGO

His eyes open.

GIACOMO

Air! The window.

UGO

Lean on me.

(*Ugo leads Giacomo to the window toward the right,
where he leans out. A pause.*)

GIACOMO

Niece.

PELLEGRINA

Uncle.

GIACOMO

There is nothing stirring there?

UGO

I can hear nothing.

PELLEGRINA
(*sullenly*)
Nothing.

GIACOMO

But I bade you

Bring cordial!

[64]

UGO

Here it is.

GIACOMO

        I bade you bring
Cordial—and yonder sits my messenger
Under the stable-lamps.

UGO

        He is sick still.

GIACOMO

Niece, I shall not forget you.   Madam, good night.

UGO

Let me go with you.

GIACOMO

        I am well I thank you.

PARISINA

Ugo!

UGO

    'Tis late. Good night, madam.
    (*Ugo goes out with Giacomo.*)

PELLEGRINA

             He's right.
Will you not go to bed?

PARISINA

        Oh, as you will,
Seeing my own will is denied by all.
    (*She sits and lets down her hair.*)

PELLEGRINA

You are weary with this journey. Would to God
Your lord had never sent us. What have we
To do in Rimini?
    (*She begins to comb her hair.*)

[65]

PARISINA

It is my home.
I think I have been happy nowhere else.

PELLEGRINA

You are forgetting, madam—

PARISINA

Pray you be
More gentle.

PELLEGRINA

Did I hurt you?

PARISINA

I must suffer
More than your clumsy hands.

PELLEGRINA

Nay, you have cause
To thank me more than chide me, madam, I
Have done you service.

PARISINA

Oh, yes.

PELLEGRINA

More than you
Suspect. Already evil tongues are making
Mischief out of your kindness to the count.

PARISINA

Come, give the comb to me.

PELLEGRINA

Pardon me, no.
My uncle Ser Giacomo—listen, lady,
I dare not speak too plainly—nay, if I would

[66]

I am not sure I know what he designs;
But pray you, take my counsel. Bid Count Ugo
Leave us!

PARISINA

Wherefore? Wherefore? Answer me!

PELLEGRINA

How can I speak without offending you?
But you must pardon me for my love's sake
That urges me to hazard your affection.
The count is young, and I have seen in him
Such signs as others, seeing, might mistake,
Or evil wills pervert to your great injury.

PARISINA

Why need you falter? Is not this your meaning—
That Ugo loves me, and I him?

PELLEGRINA

I'll swear
That he loves you; and ere you take from him
The infection send him hence!

PARISINA

And what am I
That all may scold me like a child? No more
Than my lord's lady, daughter of Rimini
And princess in Ferrara! Names too poor—
D'Este and Malatesta—to secure me
From wagging idle tongues of serving-maids.

PELLEGRINA

Ah—madam—madam—

PARISINA

Oh, yes! You have stood
All night grudging obdience. When I bade you

[67]

Go, you still lingered—nay—let go my hair!
I will not have your fingers on my hair.
Nay—will you not?
(*She strikes Pellegrina in the face. Pellegrina draws
back. They stand silent.*)

                 You press me past all patience.
                    (*Silence still*)
I cannot help it if you use me so.
                    (*She begins to cry*)

PELLEGRINA
(*After a pause filled only by Parisina's weeping*)
It had been better you had ne'er been born
Than to have lived till now.

PARISINA
                 Is it my fault?
(*Pellegrina goes out by lower door on left.*)

PARISINA
Yes, past possession of my senses. Oh!
(*Lucia enters from the door through which Pellegrina
went.*)

LUCIA
What, madam!

PARISINA
           Oh, you are smiling! Oh, at last
To see a happy face,
         (*Lucia finishes plaiting her hair.*)
               Their wrinkled brows,
Thin lips, sour eyes around me all day long!
Lucia, these sad-faced folk make the world sad
That should be happy, and all happy things

[68]

Youth, morning, love, all happy gracious things
That God provides us for a little while,
All these things they make burdens. Think you not?

LUCIA

They cannot saddle sorrow upon me.

PARISINA

Why, that's true wisdom, more than I have heard
From old Giacomo and his wise kinswoman.

LUCIA

He is a merry heart. I have made oath
If once I hear him laugh to take the veil;
For that day shall be perilous near the end
Of this world, and good time to drop those sins
Which only make it worth the living in.

PARISINA

Today was like to be his last indeed.

LUCIA

How, madam?

PARISINA

Why he fainted here.

LUCIA

Giacomo?
What enemy of mankind preserved his life?

PARISINA

You do not love him?

LUCIA

Love him? Love the devil!
He set me here before him—there sat he—
And put me to my wit's end—that's not far.

[69]

But far enough to make me wish him dead—
With questions, madam, you would hardly think it—
(*checks herself*)

PARISINA

Of what?

LUCIA

Of all that passed upon the road.

PARISINA

Between whom?

LUCIA

Why—Count Ugo and yourself.

PARISINA

To what end?

LUCIA

Nay, I cannot tell you that.
But he got nothing out of me.

PARISINA

You too, then,
Know what is in their minds.

LUCIA

Nay, I know nothing.

PARISINA

Come tell me what you know!

LUCIA

Indeed I know
Nothing. I swear it.

PARISINA

Lucia, speak to me.
I am most unhappy.

[70]

LUCIA

Sweetheart, there's no power
On earth shall tear from me what I forget.
Therefore, save before God, I do know nothing.

PARISINA

I hoped for comfort from you. I must tell you.
Lucia, they say, Giacomo and his niece,
That Ugo loves me and that I love him.

LUCIA

The lying tongues! The wicked hearts! They say
That! The black calumny!

PARISINA

Does it anger you
That they think so? When I took Romei's wife
Laodamia back to him, I could not
Rejoice, seeing how her soul was loath to go.

LUCIA

Her lover was a properer man.

PARISINA

And yet
She had sinned.

LUCIA

If you can fairly call it sin
In these days when the world is old as 'tis.
'Tis many years since 'twas accounted sin
For a young wife to fool an ancient husband.

PARISINA

It is a sin.

LUCIA

Then send the count away.

[71]

PARISINA

What!—if I do not love him—?

LUCIA

You're but a child.

PARISINA

What think you you have guessed?

LUCIA

Nay, I can read
Your story: your eyes flash it when they see him,
Your mouth betrays it when he is not near—
No, not in words—

PARISINA

Do you suspect I love him?

LUCIA

I know it, madam, as your own heart knows it.

PARISINA

Yet you yourself said 'twas black calumny
In them to say it.

LUCIA

Ah! To *say* it, yes.
You are our mistress.

PARISINA

What am I to do?

LUCIA

Get rid of Ser Giacomo.

PARISINA

What!

LUCIA

Fear not.
He's old and will die easily enough.

[72]

I think Lord Niccolo will welcome grounds
For being rid of him. Therefore do you
Inform against him ere he speak of us.

PARISINA

Must love be served by murder!

LUCIA

                    Who said murder?
They kill far better every day for food.
The leather that you walk on covered bones
That cost a mother no less pains than his.
What matter, so we see it not, what day
His venom choke him?

PARISINA

                    Whither am I going?

LUCIA

And his bright eyes once closed we need not fear;
For Pellegrina loves you, and 'twere hard
If we three women could not fool a man.
We'll help you to your wish.

PARISINA

                         You speak in love,
And every word convinces me of sin,
As if when you would bless me God decreed
You should but curse.

LUCIA

                    Where is the sin in this?

PARISINA

Love is not sin but in conspiracy.
The opposition of the world had not
So hurt my love in mine own estimation
As your confederate kindness cankers it.

[73]

LUCIA

Love blossoms where the wind carries the seed.
You cannot plant it. He that sowed the hills
With forests and the fields with primroses
Scatters this too. But! keep it hid from man
That forged the first axe to cut down the trees
And later used it to support his laws.
But we'll be very secret.

PARISINA

        I am ashamed.

(*Enter Ugo*)

LUCIA

Madam, good-night.

PARISINA

Good-night.

LUCIA

           Good-night, my lord.
(*He makes no reply and she goes out.*)

UGO

You bade me speak with you.

PARISINA

         Ugo—how white
Your face is!

UGO

      For God's mercy let's be brief.
I am in hell.

PARISINA

(*Going to him*)

I love you.

[74]

UGO

You sent for me
To ask me something.

PARISINA

Do you love me?

UGO

Yes.
You know I love you.

PARISINA

There can be no hell
Where love is.

UGO

It is love alone makes hell.

PARISINA

Or heaven.

UGO

What did you wish to say to me?

PARISINA

In your arms I will tell you everything.
There I shall fear no more: but otherwise
The very words affright me. Do not put
My arms from off your neck. I am too strong—
Stronger than you because I can perceive
Happiness in the love that daunts you yet
With sick anticipations. Oh, my love.
        (*She is in his arms. He kisses her.*)
There was a world of late, outside these arms,
Where doubt and fear oppress'd me. Suddenly
It is scaled off, forgotten, like a husk,

[75]

And my soul stands shining and confident
In this brave universe of your embrace.

(*She kisses him*)

Sweet love, I know you never did contrive
The murder of my lord.

UGO

(*Starting away*)

What's this you say?
How come our minds to murder?

PARISINA

Nay, then, I know
You never did. I knew it.

UGO

Who hath set
This horror in your heart? I murder—I!

PARISINA

Giacomo said a rumour—

UGO

Of me—of me!
That I desired my father's death?

PARISINA

Nay—partly—
Partly he said himself, not without truth,
That my lord's growing old—hath not the strength
In government he had; that you being young—

UGO

(*Throwing her off*)

This he said, and you heard him out? He said
So much and is alive! And you—you tell

[76]

The tale to me! Come! What have you contrived
With him? And am I sent for to complete
The dark conspiracy against my lord?
Tell me.

PARISINA

No—no. What have I said? No—no!

UGO

You tell his story but have given it
A ghastly accent of your own. Regret.
Is't so? Oh, Christ, Christ! Have we come to this?

PARISINA

No, do not think it! God shall be my judge.
I loathed Giacomo as you now loath me
For uttering such a thought. Oh, love, believe me!
Will you not?

UGO

Oh, we are unhappy, both.
I care not to live longer. Are these few
Uneasy kisses only to be bought
By a red stealthy dagger? Let them go.
They are not worth it.

PARISINA

On my soul I swear
I never listened with consent to him.

UGO

But now the thought, bred of that villain's heart,
Is in our minds; we never can again
Be innocent.

(*She tries to embrace him: he repulses her.*)

[77]

PARISINA

You love me then no more!
Well, love's a kind of bondage, and you grow
Weary for liberty. Well. Get you gone.
I'll not reproach you.

UGO

Still a further fall,
From death to scolding. These sharp words defile
The little virtue in our love. We make
The pity of our sin ungracious; pluck
The beauty from our passion thus to chide
Like groom and scullion.

PARISINA

Oh, I am to blame.
I ask your pardon, humbly.

UGO

Not of me!
Sweet, I am with you lock'd out of all grace.

PARISINA

Then I care not, seeing you shall be with me.
I love you.

UGO

But the years that are to come
Must be provided for.

PARISINA

Let God provide
That did ordain both circumstance and time
To catch our youth.

UGO

Nay, 'tis our part to look
How we shall live henceforth. Are you content

To feed on furtive kisses, or conspire
By calendar to meet on moonless nights?
That way our love must wither and our souls
Decline upon a hideous counterfeit.

PARISINA

Let Time come on; we'll meet him as we must.
We cannot stop his coming.

UGO

         Do you never
Think of the future?

PARISINA

         Ay, and far beyond,
Into Eternity.

UGO

         But you seem to live
For the moment only.

PARISINA

         For such moments, love,
As do each one contain Eternity.

UGO

All this is little help. Naught but his death
Can free our love to happiness: and that
—That way is barred.

PARISINA

(*with great emotion*)
         Indeed I never thought
Of violence to any.

UGO

         I charge you not.

PARISINA

No, not your words—but your eyes charge me. Kiss me!
I swear I am innocent of such a thought.

(*He will not*)

UGO

We never can be innocent thereof
Having once known it.

PARISINA

Have your way. I am done.
Farewell.

(*She turns to go.*)

UGO

Ah—first forgive me.

PARISINA

As you will.

UGO

One kiss since we'll not meet on earth again.
(*She lets him kiss her*)
One more—one more!

PARISINA

Since we must part tonight
Let it be now.

UGO

Could but my lips retain
This sweet impression till I die, the sense
Of you upon my mouth forever!

PARISINA

No.
What is one kiss more in eternity.

(*She walks towards her room.*)

[80]

UGO

Say only that you still love me! Say but that!
Parisina—Parisina!

(*She passes into her room.*)

Oh, just God!

(*He staggers to a chair and falls with his head on the table. Presently he rises and moves irresolutely to the upper entrance on the left. There he pauses. He walks rapidly into Parisina's room. Pellegrina comes out of her room and listens at Parisina's door. She passes her hand over her face. She then goes to the right-hand window and leaning out whistles softly. A lance-head is thrust up and she fixes Giacomo's "deposition" upon it. She comes back into the room, listening. A horse's hoofs ring out.*)

PELLEGRINA

It had been better you had ne'er been born.

CURTAIN

ACT III.

ACT III. PARISINA

(The following night. Lucia is looking from the right-hand window. Pellegrina is seated at the table, her chin in her hands, anxious.)

LUCIA

(Yawning)

This is sleepy weather, or perhaps
A sleepy hour. The moon's up; and no sign
Of our dear travellers.

(Leans out of window)

Ho! You below—! Black eyes!
What news yet of my lady?

(A spear-head is thrust up. She catches it laughing.)

What? You want
A rose? Nay, now, you are almost a man
And hardly safe to play at roses with—
Black eyes! But lest you fall a-weeping—there!

(She fixes a rose from her bosom on the lance-point and shuts the window.)

PELLEGRINA

Can you not let them be?

LUCIA

Let whom?

PELLEGRINA

Men! Men!

[85]

LUCIA

Oh—sulking still!

PELLEGRINA

For hardly more than this
That is a jest with you, the brightest lives
Have been snuffed out.

LUCIA

Well, since the world began
Men have shed blood for women. Dogs will snarl
Over their meat. 'Tis something will not change
Till the world cools, and we can only hope
To escape it. But it were a sorry life
That stole a tip-toe through a world of fears
And grudged the price of pleasure, when, with luck,
One might enjoy it and not pay at all.

PELLEGRINA

Fate hath no menace for such hearts as yours.
You babble of death as 'twere so far away
You should have years of warning ere it come.
But I can see them—love and death—divided
But by a sudden question.

LUCIA

Oh, I know
What you would say. I have seen the twain you hint at.
And listen! With your cloudy face you threaten
Rain while the world is sunny. Tell me this!
Since when was it a vice in Italy
To fool a doting husband?

(*Enter Niccolo from outside, with Giacomo.*)

[86]

NICCOLO

(*As Lucia shrinks towards Parisina's door.*)
                        Stay, you, mistress!
Giacomo! Let no soul escape from here.
(*Giacomo goes out again. There is a grim pause till he
    returns.*)
                                            Now!
I stand unready to believe the word
That brought me hither. See you make it good!

GIACOMO

It shall be proved.

NICCOLO
                    That were best for you all.

GIACOMO

Oh, sir, I shall convince you.

NICCOLO
                            It shall be hard;
Yet see you do it. This you have begun
Must find a swift conclusion: yes, tonight!
For I and this suspicion cannot live
Another day together. You have spread
Poison that hath infected the same air
You must yourself breathe; and you have incurred
An equal liability to the plague
They are suspected of. Come now! See to it!
Lips and eyes God gave us, and we count
Those folk unhappy that be dumb or blind.
But some there be shall wish they had been born
Eyeless and speechless if I shall discover
Their eyes or lips deceived in their report,
And these twain innocent whom they accuse.

GIACOMO

My lord, I have no fear but I can prove it.

NICCOLO

(*Spreading out the deposition*)

I have read this deposition and can find
No evil in it. Does that daunt you now?
You, mistress, that have signed this paper here,
—Is this your name—here by the dagger's mark—

(*Lucia looks fearfully at the paper and nods.*)

What does this mean to you?

(*She is silent*)

GIACOMO

Speak, Lucia! Speak!

LUCIA

(*screaming*)

Before eternal God—!

NICCOLO

So stand we all!
And nearer now before God's burning face
Than ever consciously stood living soul.
I charge you all that you do make no speed
To meet your maker, for by God I swear
Some are to die tonight. I'll wait. I'll wait.

(*There is a pause: Niccolo paces up and down. Lucia sways.*)

Give her a chair.

(*Giacomo does so*)

Be not too careful neither.

Now take no thought to be on either side
In this determination. Right and wrong
Were ne'er so clean divided as tonight.

Speak what you know. They that I find guilty
Shall pay. But if the charge be proven false
It is too late by silence to escape
The count of calumny—since here's your name.

(*Lucia collapses*)

Take her away and lock the door upon her.

(*Giacomo leads her past the table towards the door of
her room. As they pass Pellegrina Lucia calls out.*)

LUCIA

Pellegrina!

NICCOLO

Nay! You are in the awful hand
Of justice, which is God's. No human soul
Can bear your burden.

(*Giacomo locks her into her room. Niccolo addresses
Pellegrina.*)

What have you to say?

PELLEGRINA

I think Lord Ugo loves my lady.

NICCOLO

Fool!

I know it! And she him. And both of them
I love, and God I hope loves all of us.
What is the sin here?

PELLEGRINA

In the way of sin
I think my lord and lady love each other

NICCOLO

(*Referring to the paper*)

This is your name?

[89]

PELLEGRINA

It is.

NICCOLO

This paper carries
The evidence supporting your suspicion?

PELLEGRINA

It does.

NICCOLO

I see no crime in it. Mark this!
"At first my lord rode by my lady's side.
His head was bowed. He did not speak at all.
My lady sought to cheer him but in vain."
Well—what of this?

PELLEGRINA

I do not stand by that,
Though to discerning eyes—

NICCOLO

Suspicious eyes,
Evil-intending—

PELLEGRINA

Since upon my words
My life or death depend I may demand
My words be heard and not distorted by
The passions of my judge.

NICCOLO

Go on, go on!

PELLEGRINA

Then, to discerning eyes most manifestly
The manner of my lord betrayed his heart.

[90]

NICCOLO

Why, what is this but your interpretation.
What value has it?

GIACOMO

Pray you, sir, read on.

NICCOLO

"After we left the town he fell behind.
Twice she sent for him but he would not come."
Indeed this passion seems not over bold
That twice refuses opportunity.
(*Pellegrina smiles*)
What—do you smile?

GIACOMO

That is the very mark
Of guilty lovers.

NICCOLO

What know you of love?

PELLEGRINA

My uncle's right.

GIACOMO

(*Reading over Niccolo's shoulder*)
"My lady grieved at this."

NICCOLO

So well she might—and so had I, to feel
The least estrangement from him. Here again,
On entering the inn "My lady sent
Once more to bring him to her; still in vain.
At this she wept." Now for the twentieth time
I read this paper and am more convinced
That these two souls are innocent, and you
Practiced against them for some villainous end.

[91]

GIACOMO

Why 'tis apparent.

NICCOLO

What appears in it?

GIACOMO

That conscious of his guilt the count refused
To see my lady.

NICCOLO

Should a messenger
Bright out of Heaven declare the same to me
Upon no other evidence than this,
I would not credit him. How then shall you,
Stain'd with three decades of conspiracy,
Or this pale wench convince me? Here I read
That my son Ugo, whom against his will
I sent upon this journey, had no mind
To cloud my lady's presence with his wrath.
She, loving him, as I rejoice to know,
Sought to console him: but he still refrained.

GIACOMO

And all that evening she was ill-at-ease;
Unhappy—weeping often; and my lord
Only with difficulty was persuaded
By me to come to her.

NICCOLO

Which proves the more
That so far from desiring it, he sought
But to avoid her presence.

GIACOMO

Which but proves
Too plainly that he feared to be with her.

Why all this day the twain have been together—
Are not returned yet.

NICCOLO
                    Why then—where's the fear
Today that kept them yesternight apart?
You are sore put to it. May not my wife and son
Walk in the fields without suspicion? No!
I am not satisfied.

GIACOMO
                    I'll say no more.
You are determined to discredit me.
Come—take my head and live among the lies
That please you better than the sour-faced truths
I ever served you with.

NICCOLO
(*weakened*)
                    Nay—Wait! One moment!
What have you *seen?*

GIACOMO
(*smiling*)
                    My lord, what should I see?
What more than we *have* seen and is told here
Could any hope to see? What action note
More than by inference from their eyes and voices,
Their starts and changing colour? If you ask
The tale of their embraces, kisses—these
I have not seen, and must in this default
Endure your utmost anger.

NICCOLO
                    God defend you.
"Last night," you said?

[93]

GIACOMO

Not I, I'll say no more.

NICCOLO

"Last night" is in my brain—ringing—ringing!
Who set these syllables clashing within me?
(*to Pellegrina*)
Speak, woman! put a meaning on these words!
What's come upon us when our common speech
Grows dark with rumours from the abyss of Fate,
And words of household use, the cheap exchange,
Toll like the sentence of a Sybil's tongue
Pronouncing doom. "Last night!" Give this a meaning!

GIACOMO

If you should shrink—

NICCOLO

I have heard *you*. Prompt her not!

PELLEGRINA

If he imply that he saw anything
More than has been disclosed, my uncle lies.

GIACOMO

I claimed no more.

NICCOLO

We are coming to the truth.
Prepare your souls.

PELLEGRINA

I only saw—

NICCOLO

Be certain!

[94]

PELLEGRINA

I saw lord Ugo enter her bed-chamber;—
And though I watched the night away till dawn
I saw him not depart.

NICCOLO

(after a pause)

If I have fought
Against my own heart's jealousy so long
A winning battle, why should I confess
Suddenly at this woman's word, defeat?
Well, then, I have been wrong these many years.
I have lived swaddled in illusions—now
They scatter and above my dream arises
The sun, a globe of blood. In blood were laid
The bricks that built Ferrara; in the blood
Of kinsmen was my seat established there;
In blood was I to that succession born.
Then nothing's strange here. I accept the world
That I was born to.
                        When my lady comes
Do you attend her! Let none know I am here!
When you have left my lady in her bed
Show yonder candle from the window-sill;
And if you loved her, say "farewell." Keep then
In your own room. If you love virtue, honour,
Faith, charity and hope—there cut your throat,
Or be resolved to live without them here.

(Half to Giacomo)

I am returned to a familiar world
And walk sure-footed.
                        Come now, bite your lips
Lest she observe their pallour. We must meet

[95]

The world with our old faces, and forget
Kindliness and affection and all peace,
Which are the sport of villains and the grief
Of God and saints that must despair of men.

(*Niccolo goes out. Giacomo opens the door of Lucia's room.*)

GIACOMO

Come hither!

(*Enter Lucia*)

LUCIA

I am innocent, I swear!
What does he mean to do? What does he think?
Who told him aught?

PELLEGRINA

(*as if to herself*)

She never should have struck me.

LUCIA

Was it you betrayed her?

PELLEGRINA

Nay, her own hand sealed
Her sentence.

GIACOMO

Come! You are not to be seen here.

LUCIA

What's to be done?

GIACOMO

No harm to you. My lord
Hath here regained his wits and I can see
The features of the good old time again.
Delay no more, I say!

(*He takes her out.*)

[96]

PELLEGRINA

(*After a bitter pause*)

I have brought back
The buried times of wrath and cruelty.
It had been better I had ne'er been born.

(*Parisina and Ugo enter together. Parisina runs and
embraces Pellegrina.*)

PARISINA

Oh, I am sorry I offended you—
Indeed, indeed! Pray you forgive me, dear,
And be my friend again. I dare not raise
My head from your soft heart till you have said
"Yes, I forgive you." Say it. Do not make
My penance longer than I have endured,
Remembering my unkindness. Say it! Why,
My anger could not last so long.

PELLEGRINA

(*brokenly*)

I do

Forgive you.

PARISINA

Then the world is bright again
That lack'd but this to perfect its delight.
Oh, the fair things we have seen! Would you believe,
Pellegrina, that the violets are out,
Pansy and primrose—all the world's awake
So early, and the light dappling the land
Between the forest branches. I am pleased
With this world. It contents me.

PELLEGRINA

Are you not

Weary?

PARISINA

    What white lips! Were my lips so pale
I'd bite them till the blood came back again
Lest men should—well—red lips are better loved.

UGO

You will be pale too if you take no rest.

PARISINA

I think I shall sleep sound. And none but you
Shall wait on me, Pellegrina.
   (*Pellegrina goes into Parisina's room. To Ugo*)
                   Do not go.
          (*She embraces him.*)
I love you.

UGO

           Wonderful, oh, wonderful!

PARISINA

And yesterday, but only yesterday
How far apart were we? That is a day
You have cut from our lives.

UGO

           I?

PARISINA

                None but you,
Who most had reason—yet not more than I—
To cherish every hour allowed to us.

UGO

But yesterday before your kiss had healed
My heart by love and duty wounded—oh,
Sweet soul, I dared not speak to you.

[98]

PARISINA

What, dared not!
You are bold enough now.

UGO

For your lips have set me
Above the lists where men wrestle with Fate.
Below me in the dust I hear them cry
"Honour," "peace," "happiness," "reason," and "God"
Which signify to me—nothing. And twice
You sent for me.

PARISINA

Nay, thrice! I have not forgotten,
Albeit you are forgiven.

UGO

Well, then, thrice!
And there was consolation in the pain
I had, refusing you. For oh, my soul
Was dark for you—and all the glitter and stir,
Murmur and clatter of the cavalcade,
Threshed through my aching senses one refrain,
Parisina, Parisina, Parisina.

PARISINA

And there was I.

UGO

But in despair I dashed
This music into pieces, and awoke
Out of that dark world throbbing in my soul,
And plunged among the happier elements
Of grooms and men-at-arms, to learn of them
A grosser way of love that should not rack
And torture memory. With them I shouted

[99]

Vile songs and gloried in the degradation
Our lips made of this passion that devoured
My peace for you.

PARISINA

But why? Was I not there?

UGO

Ay, but not then for me. My wound was bleeding.
For 'tis not the obscenest lust that kills,
But love; and could I smirch my love for you
I had recovered from it. So together
We drank and diced, the horseboys and the heir
Of old Ferrara. But in vain. I loved you
With a fixed passion sombre as the grave
And not more easily to be escaped.

PARISINA

Oh, you have suffered!

UGO

I have fought in vain.
I am defeated. What shall come of it?

PARISINA

Defeated! I do not regard it so.
Defeated? I have won from adverse Fate
Some certain moments of a perfect joy.
God hath no scourge to lash from memory
The thing that is between us. Come the host
Of saints and martyrs to confound my shame,
I love you.

UGO

Oh, rebellion on your lips
Even against God doth enchant my senses.
I wonder you are not afriad.

[100]

PARISINA

I fear
One thing only.

UGO

What, must you whisper it?

PARISINA

(*whispering*)
Lest you that lately held me in your arms
Should cease to love the memory.

UGO

God forget me
If I delight not in it till my death.

PARISINA

Nay—after death.

UGO

If we have memory still
This shall be my delight in burning hell.

PARISINA

Then we are happy. Oh, so happy now
I could face death and laugh. Could you not now
Contemplate death, Ugo, and not repine,
Having so bright a recent memory
As maybe life should never bring again?

UGO

Will you play now with death? Are you so bold
To dance upon the grave that waits for all?

PARISINA

Yes, surely, being armed with happiness
I do not fear to face unhappy things.
Think! Might we now, this instant, quietly
Die on the selfsame breath! That were a way

[101]

To cheat this difficult, deceitful world.
And none should sorrow then.

UGO

                              Sweet, do not call
On death. O beauty, can you wish to die?

PARISINA

For if we shed this lovely, troubled flesh,
We might be joined for ever without sin,
Since if we sinned we sinned but in the flesh
That's mortal and with death shall be forgot.
But this our love's not mortal, but shall be
Our joy hereafter. Then I do not fear
Death. Let it come upon me when it will,
So we be not divided. And this faith
Absolves me now before I come to die,
Being not unready to accept the pains,
The brief wounds of mortality.

UGO

                              By God!
I would not give thy body unto death.
Nay, talk no more of it!

PARISINA

                    Not even in scorn?

UGO

Imperishable should your beauty be,
But since 'tis mortal—charm away once more
The thought of what awaits it.

PARISINA
(*kissing him*)

                              Life and death
Are in eternity united here

[102]

Where in our kiss eternity is caught.

(Pellegrina comes back from Parisina's room carrying a small ewer and basin.)

UGO

We talk of time and of eternity,
And quite forget the necessary hour
When we shall start tomorrow.

PARISINA

Nay, but let us
Remain one day more. Shall we? How your hands
Tremble, Pellegrina!

(She washes her hands)

PELLEGRINA

They are cold, I think.

PARISINA

You are not vexed still with me?

PELLEGRINA

Madam—no.

PARISINA

Dear Pellegrina.

PELLEGRINA

Do not stay: begone
As early as you may, and if you may—
To-night! Wait not for morning: Will you—Will you?

PARISINA

Why, what is this?

(Giacomo enters. Pellegrina drops the basin.)

PELLEGRINA

(frantically)
Pardon me—Oh, pardon!

[103]

PARISINA

Come, there's no harm done.

(*Pellegrina goes out with the things*)

GIACOMO

Ah, you are waking yet.

PARISINA

Do you need me?

GIACOMO

Only to ask you, madam,
What hour you'll ride tomorrow.

PARISINA

We were speaking
This very moment of it, and Count Ugo
Said that I chattered of eternity
And never thought of Time.

GIACOMO

True piety
Keeps its eye ever on the life to come
And lets this world go by.

PARISINA

Well, we'll not go
Tomorrow—nor maybe the next day neither.

(*Re-enter Pellegrina. She starts, but is silenced by a look from Giacomo.*)

I like this place.

GIACOMO

Well, that is fortunate,
Since I've bad news I fear for you, my lord.

UGO

What should that be?

[104]

GIACOMO

Your chestnut that you love
Has fallen lame; over-ridden I fear.

UGO

My father's gift! I'd not have had this happen.

GIACOMO

Will you come look at her?

PARISINA

Ay—do! Make haste!
Poor beauty! And but yesterday so proud.

UGO

Where is she?

GIACOMO

In the stable. I'll go with you.

PARISINA

You will come back and tell me her condition?
I'd gladly hear she was not much in pain.

UGO

I will come back if it be not too late
When I have done what may be done for her.
But if I see you not, sleep you well, madam.

GIACOMO

I fear it will be late.
(*They go out*)

PARISINA
(*running to the window towards the left*)
Good-night.

UGO
(*from below*)
Good-night.

PARISINA

I do not like to see a beast in pain.

PELLEGRINA

These tears but for a horse?

PARISINA

Poor thing—poor thing!
I am happy, Pellegrina,
And cannot bear to think the whole wide world
Is not as happy in its meanest life
As I am. Were I God I should decree
An end to pain. Then there'd be no more sin,

PELLEGRINA

How does that follow?

PARISINA

I would have it so,
Were I God. I'll not sleep yet.

PELLEGRINA

Very well.

PARISINA

How's this? You do not chide me? You were wont
To chide me when I would not do your will.

PELLEGRINA

'Tis not my will.

PARISINA

I think you do not chide
Because last night I was unkind to you,
Which you repay me with indulgence now,
And in good sooth I am in need of it.
Be good to me, Pellegrina.

(*She cries on her breast*)

[106]

PELLEGRINA

                    Is *this* happiness?
You were so happy!

PARISINA

                    Well, I like to weep
Now you are here to wipe my tears away.
Indeed I am happy, dear.

PELLEGRINA

                    What shall I do?

PARISINA

Kiss me and I will dry them.

PELLEGRINA

                    (*drying her eyes*)
                              There, there, there.
Weep no more.

PARISINA

                    Nay, but kiss me and I will not.
                    (*Pellegrina kisses her.*)
Now I'll remember all the happy hours
And pleasant things that have made life for me.
If all thing pass 'tis labour lost to weep
For sorrow.   Grief and pain do not endure;
Love only endures, doth it not, Pellegrina?

PELLEGRINA

Yes.

PARISINA

                    I believe it.   But sometimes I feel
I am at war with Time and this harsh world;
And therefore cannot but endure defeat,
Since Time and this world wear all things away.

Then I remember love and instantly
I chide myself for this faint heart of mine,
And bind this world to be my friend, defying
Time that is but the lackey of my heart
Making that love which in my heart abides
Richer in memory and in promise too.
Oh, yes, I am happy.

               You are tired, sweet friend.
I do you wrong to keep you from your bed.
Then I will sleep now.

PELLEGRINA

    Indeed, I am not weary.

PARISINA

I must not task the kindness of my friends,
Of whom you are the first. Why do you look so?
You know how well I love you.

    (*She holds out her hand to her*)

                  Oh, some day
God will repent—

PELLEGRINA

    Sweetheart, that's blasphemy—

PARISINA

But surely He will find some way to help
Unhappy people. I know I have not loved
His name enough since it is used to fright us
From all we most desire. But I'm a child
And have, I know, most foolish ignorant thoughts
On such deep things. Oh, but I've a secret
To tell you when the world is bright again,
As it will be in good time—in God's time
Who hath these days a little darkened it,
My sweet friend, sister.

[108]

PELLEGRINA

I can bear no more.
The end must come.

PARISINA

I knew I wearied you.
Come, I'll to bed.

(*Pellegrina lights a candle*)

I know that with the sun
The sorrow of the night shall disappear.

(*They pass into her bedroom. Presently Pellegrina comes back and stands, hesitating to place the candle in the window. Before she makes up her mind Parisina re-enters.*)

I will not sleep in there. The moonlight strikes
Upon my pillow, and you have often told me
That is unlucky. Pray you, let me sleep
Here, on this couch.

(*Pellegrina goes to fetch sheets and pillows from the other room.*)

Oh, drowsy as I am
I still make trouble for you.

(*While Pellegrina settles her on the couch*)

Did you not say
That moonlight on a sleeper brings ill-luck?

PELLEGRINA

Then 'twas in idleness, for light or dark
There's no avoiding fate.

PARISINA

Ah, leave the candle!
I fear the moonlight and the darkness too,

But that's a kind, companionable beam
Of man's invention. Set it over there.
(*Pellegrina laughs.*)

PARISINA
(*drowsily*)
Why do you laugh?

PELLEGRINA
Oh, I have caught a glimpse
Of a divine diversion where the puppets
Have from God's anxious fingers snatched the strings
And utter with their painted mouths the speeches
That bring the action to the end prepared.
(*She sets the candle in the window*)
Come then! Come soon!

PARISINA
(*sleepily*)
What are you murmuring.

PELLEGRINA
(*turning out the lamp*)
Farewell.
(*She waits for a reply: then goes toward her own
room.*)
Parisina!
(*No reply*)
Better I had ne'er been born,
But having lived till now, I may amend
The vice of living.
(*She goes into her room. Presently Niccolo enters
with a drawn sword in his hand. He takes the candle
and is moving twoard Parisina's room when he sees*

her sleeping. He stands motionless. The curtain
falls for a moment to indicate the lapse of some
hours. When it rises he is still standing with the
sword in one hand and the candle, now guttering
to extinction in the other.)

NICCOLO

I have delayed too long. My resolution
Hath lit me through but half of my design,
And dies now like this flame. I have stayed too long.

(*He blows out the light.*)

It had been little then; now what remains
Daunts me.
           Oh! You sleep well. 'Twere merciful
Now to secure thee in that sounder sleep
Without the sudden pang of dissolution.
I would have mercy on thee—so much mercy
To spare what pains I may. And still my arm
Is weighed upon by sense of that remorse
Which justice could not soothe. Can I go back?
And carry through my brief declining winter
This evil hidden from the common eye,
As one that smiles to cover his disease
Till it destroy him?
           Is all this a lie,
That gentle and undreaming sleep of hers?
The scornful purity of those shut eyes?
Why, what a fool am I to look for that
Which all the world conspired to hide from me.
Who shall convict her if not I myself,
That most have cause to keep myself deceived?
I will believe this sleep is innocent.

[111]

PARISINA
(*waking*)

Ugo!

NICCOLO

So now! We are awake once more!

PARISINA

How came you in? Who's there?

NICCOLO

                                No lover, madam,
But I, your fool—your husband. Is it strange
To find him in your bed-chamber? A pity,
But nothing out of order.

PARISINA

                Oh, my lord!
I never thought that you—

NICCOLO

                Too pale, my lady,
Why do you look so pale? This moonlight turns
The whole world ghostly. Yet 'tis not so long
Since you flushed red enough beneath his kiss.
How should I know? Why, 'tis the common way
Of lovers—we remember—even we,
The old men and the husbands, how we played.
Come, colour up! I have a bridegroom for you.
'Tis not your time yet to appear so white;
When 'tis you shall not flush again.

PARISINA

                        What's this?

NICCOLO

I will not hear you.

[112]

PARISINA

If you intend my death
You *must* hear me.

NICCOLO

Your voice!

PARISINA

Oh, now I see
Your purpose is yet molten in your mind,
Not hardened to destroy me. Why, what's this?
Someone hath practised on your mind against me—

NICCOLO

I will not hear you speak. I knew you would
Defend yourself with lies. Such souls as these
Lack not for vindication of soft speeches
To stagger justice in a heart disarmed.

PARISINA

Nay, if you prate of justice I've a right
To hearing.

NICCOLO

Briefly, briefly then.

PARISINA

I am cold.

NICCOLO

It is no matter.

PARISINA

Niccolo—my lord—

NICCOLO

Oh, speak, speak, speak!

PARISINA

What do you charge me with?

NICCOLO

Adultery.

PARISINA

With whom?

NICCOLO

Count Ugo.

PARISINA

Let
My woman Pellegrina witness for me
That sleeps in yonder chamber—and so lightly
She must know all that passed. Pellegrina!
        (*Niccolo goes to Pellegrina's room*)

NICCOLO

Hither,
Woman, and give your evidence again.
        (*He opens the door and looks in*)
Ha! Ha! You have done wisely!—look you, madam,
Here's testimony—from one that sleeps more sound
Than you believed.

PARISINA

(*Looking into the room*)
Dead!

NICCOLO

Here's grim evidence!
What further witness will you call?

PARISINA

I'll say
Nothing till you do face me with the man
I am accused with.

[114]

NICCOLO

(*calling*)

Giacomo!

PARISINA

Give me leave

To clothe myself, I pray you.

NICCOLO

Wherefore—wherefore?

PARISINA

I am cold.

NICCOLO

What's that to thee who even now
Stand on the brink of everlasting fire?

(*Enter Giacomo*)

Two things. Let word be carried to Ferrara
For that foul harlot's death I late redeemed
To virtue and her lord. Oh, she had eyes,
The laughing harlot, to perceive such things
As we poor innocent folk could dream not of.

GIACOMO

Laodamia Romei?

NICCOLO

Even she.

Then bring Count Ugo hither, as he is.

GIACOMO

Hither, my lord?

NICCOLO

Oh! here's thy just man, God.

(*kneels*)

[115]

And as for one just man thou wouldst have spared
Sodom, spare us the issue of our sins!
For this man's sake who only in thy sight
Is amiable, beseech Thee!

GIACOMO

Good my lord—

NICCOLO

(*leaping up*)

Answer me not! What's death that I should stay
My hand on any that restrain'd me now?

(*Exit Giacomo. There is a silence. Then Parisina
speaks as if to herself.*)

PARISINA

When we came through the gate, seven years ago,
Into Ferrara on my bridal day,
He came to meet me. 'Twas you sent him out
To greet me in your name. And he wore white.
That was a sunny morning and the rays
Lit his fair hair and winked and glittered on
His silver trappings. But behind the moat
Amid the castle-shadows you abode
My coming, clad in crimson and in gold.
Why did you send him to me?

NICCOLO

There was none
On earth I loved so much.

PARISINA

Often we sat
Together in a window-seat and read
Old tales; and you came oft and watched us there,
Yet could not in imagination mix,

[116]

As we did, with the folk we read of. Why
Suffer'd you thus our fancies to be joined?
You should have set the seas between us twain;
Wide continents and arméd nations placed
To make irreconcilable divorce
Between us. But you did not. Nay, you smiled
To see the bond unite us every day
More closely—even the bond which now you seek
To sever with the sword.

                    NICCOLO
                    It is in vain
To cast on me the shadow of your guilt.

                    PARISINA
Then in your heart I am condemned already,
No witnesses—no pleader—no defence?

                    NICCOLO
All these have spoken for you in my heart:
And have been answered.

                    PARISINA
        (*She throws herself at his feet*)
                    Bid them speak again!
Have pity.

                    NICCOLO
                Pity! In my bosom burnt
A love for you that made the house it lodged in
Unfit for frailer feeling. That fire's out
And the place ashy.
            (*She falls weeping to the floor*)
                    I forget that life
When your tears might have moved me. Now my soul

Observes with awe this tenantless abode
My body, that no sense cries out in it
To see you sorrowing.

(*Giacomo enters with men bearing the body of Ugo
d'Este. They lay him on the table. He is in his
shirt and the wound of his death shows red on it.
He is covered with mire and straw from the stable.
Parisina rises.*)

NICCOLO

            You shall have but time
To make confession for you are to die.

PARISINA

No, I'll not make confession. There's no priest
Can help me, for of this that I have done
I never can repent. Slay me, Lord Niccolo.

NICCOLO

Repent, repent, for you must die. Repent!
There is no hope for you.

PARISINA

            Nay, not in life;
Since he is dead. Sweet lover, I repent
Only that such sweet kisses were so few.
Come now, let justice, virtue, envy and wrath
Wreak their despite upon this body of mine,
For their worst hatred shall but serve my will.
I do embrace the sword.

(*Niccolo stabs her. She falls.*)

NICCOLO

Thou'st chosen well.

[118]

Jesu! Ugo!

(She dies)

NICCOLO

Throw out these bodies naked on the street
That all may see the marriage.

GIACOMO

     Sir—sir—justice
Is executed—

NICCOLO

*(He has picked some of the straw from the dead
 youth's head.)*
     Justice shall content
Offended honour—not a heart abused—
Not love corrupted. Strip them! Crown them both
With straw out of the stable—bridal chaplets—
Oh! they are beautiful.
       I'll cover them.
I am an old man and in my house
The young are dead.

CURTAIN

www.ingramcontent.com/pod-product-compliance
Lightning Source LLC
Chambersburg PA
CBHW020151180626
46810CB00004B/1842